YOUNG EXPLORERS

A FAMILY SECRET

Place SUCCESS BADGE here! Read page 73 to learn how to get it.

SOLVED

Written by B. Vitale and J. I. Wagner. Illustrated by J. G. Ratti. Edited by T. Phua.

All rights reserved. Copyright 2020 by J. I. Wagner. Published by freshabooks. freshabooks is an imprint of: freshamedia GmbH, Robert-Bosch-Str. 32, 63303 Dreieich, Germany.

www.timmitobbson.com | www.freshabooks.com

ISBN 978-3963267307

Printed 2021 in the United States of America.

Certified Chain of Custody
SUSTAINABLE FORESTRY INITIATIVE
Promoting Sustainable Forestry
www.sfiprogram.org
SFI-01268

SFI label applies to the text stock

Hi. I'm Timmi.

I may not be the most confident boy. Or the most athletic. Or the best at anything. But I *am* quite curious. That seems to be good.

This is Lilli.

She can be stubborn.

And sassy.

But above all, she is the bravest and boldest person I know. She'd do anything to help you.

This is Marvin.

He loves animals.

Whenever he gets excited,

he bobs up and down on

the spot. And he claps.

It looks silly, but he doesn't care.

This is the story of how we three came

to be known as the **Young Explorers**.

Pssst. Here is a secret mission.

The seven images shown below can each be found on the following pages! Search for them and note the page number you found them on. Then go to timmitobbson.com and find the secret area. Enter the page numbers to pass the security check. A surprise awaits you!

Find:

Found on page:

A FAMILY SECRET

FACTS
FOR EXPLORERS

HANDBOOK
FOR EXPLORERS

WRITING IN THE MARGINS

Late one evening, I heard a knock on my door. It was my older brother Tom.

"Listen," he said. "I have to tell you something important."

I could see he was serious.

"Tomorrow is your class trip to the library, right?" Tom asked.

I nodded.

"Okay. What I am about to tell you must remain a secret. You can tell Lilli and Marvin, but no one else. Can I count on you?" he asked.

"Of course. I promise," I said.

"In the library, each kid will be given a very old book to look at," Tom said.

"I know," I said. "They warned us to be really careful with the books."

"Right. Now, one of these books is special. It holds a secret message."

"A secret message? What are you talking about?" I asked.

Tom shook his head. "I can't tell you more right now. But you need to find the book and follow its clues."

With that, Tom got up and left. I could hardly sleep that night. What secret message was my brother talking about?

The next morning I met up with my two best friends, Lilli and Marvin. On our way to the library, I told them what had happened.

"A secret message?" Marvin asked, eyes wide. "Maybe a treasure map."

"No way," said Lilli. "I bet it's a prank."

I shrugged. "Let's find the book, okay?"
My friends nodded. A little later, we met
our class in the library reading area.
"You each have before you an ancient
book," said the librarian, Mrs. Wiseone.
I looked down at mine and wondered if
it held the secret.

Mrs. Wiseone saw me and scowled. "Timmi Tobbson," she said. "Are you listening?"

"Sorry," I said.

Mrs. Wiseone nodded. "As I was saying, these books must be handled with care. Turn the pages slowly. They may break!"

Around me, pages started turning. Suddenly, I heard Lilli's voice. "Your frog?" she whispered. "You brought your three-legged frog?"

Some time ago, Marvin had found a frog. It was hurt, and he'd helped it get better. I knew Marvin wanted to take it to the vet later that day.

The frog was in a special

box the vet had given Marvin.

"I didn't want Froggy to be lonely,"

Marvin said.

"Lonely?" Lilli said. "It's a FROG!"

Fourteen heads turned to look at Lilli.

Lilli's eyes grew wide. She'd yelled in the

library! Even *I* knew that wasn't allowed.

Mrs. Wiseone walked over to us.

"What was that about a—"

14

She stopped short. "Marvin," she shouted. "These books are part of a rare collection. And you would *dare* underline words?"

Marvin looked puzzled. He glanced down at the book. "It wasn't me!"

"Don't you lie to me," Mrs. Wiseone said. She pointed at Marvin's drawings below the book. "You've been drawing in pencil, and the words in the book are underlined in pencil too."

I knew Marvin would never write in an antique book. Lilli and I stood to get a better look.

Three words were underlined. But there was something strange about one of the lines.

"Marvin didn't do it," I said. "The words were underlined a long time ago."

The solution to each puzzle is revealed at the beginning of the following chapter. You can find hints at the back of this book.

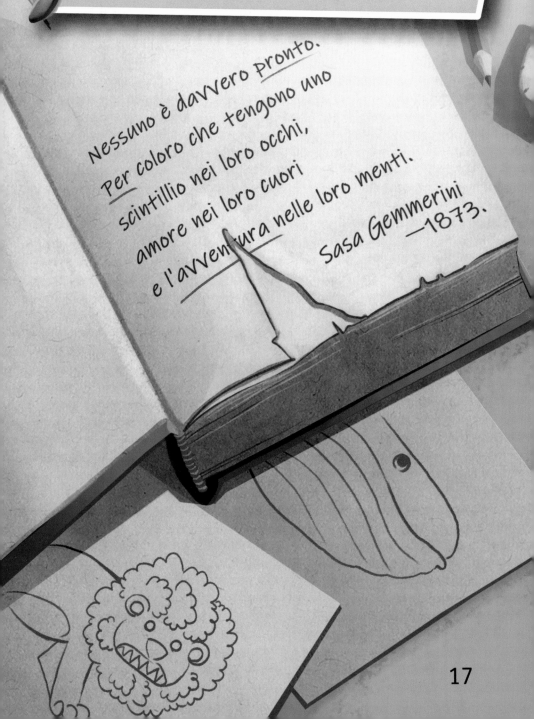

What little detail made me think the lines were old?

Nessuno è davvero pronto.
Per coloro che tengono uno
scintillio nei loro occhi,
amore nei loro cuori
e l'avventura nelle loro menti.

Sasa Gemmerini
—1873.

SECRET MESSAGES

I pointed to the tear in the page. "If Marvin had drawn the line, there would be color on the page below. But there isn't."

Mrs. Wiseone looked closely. "You're right. I apologize," she said.

Marvin grinned. "It's okay. I forgive you."

I looked at the page. "What do the underlined words mean?"

"They mean 'ready for adventure'," said
Marvin, clapping his hands.

"How do you know that?" Lilli asked.

Marvin shrugged. "My grandfather is
Italian," he said.

Ready for adventure, I thought. *This
could be one of the clues my brother
told me about.*

"Are there more markings?" I asked.

Mrs. Wiseone slowly turned the pages.

"No," she said and turned the book over.

"But this is volume one of three."

"So there are more books like this?" I

asked. "Can you help us find the others?"

Mrs. Wiseone led us into a sparsely lit back room. "This is where we keep the rare books."

She scanned a shelf. "Ah, yes. Here we are. Volumes two and three."

Mrs. Wiseone opened the second book. It had markings, too.

"Trova il mostro," I read.

"Find the monster," Marvin said.

"Monster?" I asked. "Are you sure?"

He nodded. For a brief moment, no one dared speak.

"Let's try the last book," Lilli said finally.

Mrs. Wiseone opened it.

"Posari i libri," Marvin read. "Lay the books down."

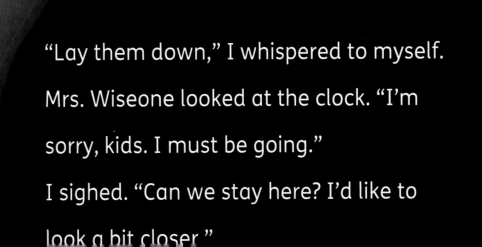

"Lay them down," I whispered to myself.

Mrs. Wiseone looked at the clock. "I'm

sorry, kids. I must be going."

I sighed. "Can we stay here? I'd like to

look a bit closer."

I watched Mrs. Wiseone's face. I could tell she didn't know if she could trust us. Finally, she smiled.

"Okay, you may stay. I misjudged you before. Let this be my apology. But please, be careful."

As soon as she left, we examined the books.

"Where are we supposed to find this monster?" I asked.

"There must be another clue," Marvin said, carefully flipping pages.

Suddenly Lilli gasped. "Wait a minute! That's it!"

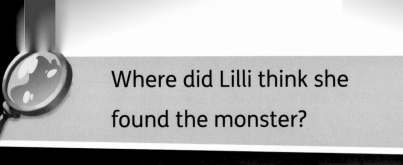

Where did Lilli think she found the monster?

THE FOUR BEASTS

Lilli put the books next to each other.

The lines on the spines came together to

make a picture.

"That's it!" she said again. "That must be

the monster!"

"Lilli," I said. "You're a genius!"

Marvin tilted his head. "Looks cute."

"Guys!" Lilli said. "I've seen this before!"

Grabbing the books, she took off.

I looked at Marvin and shrugged. "I

guess we follow her?" I said.

He nodded, and we dashed after her.

We followed Lilli up some long, winding stairs. We had to tread softly. The library was a quiet place. We did not want to draw attention to ourselves.

We found Lilli peering over the railing.

"Look," she said. "The four statues down there look like our monster."

Lilli was right!

"And in front of each statue is some sort of tray," she said excitedly.

Lilli repeated the secret message. "Find the monster. Lay the books down."

"So we have to lay the books on one of the trays?" I asked.

"Yes!" Marvin said. "Maybe a secret door will open if we get it right."

"But these statues look the same," I said.

Marvin leaned over the railing. "No, they don't," he said. "Only one matches the statue on the spines of the books."

Which statue matches the one on the spines of the books?

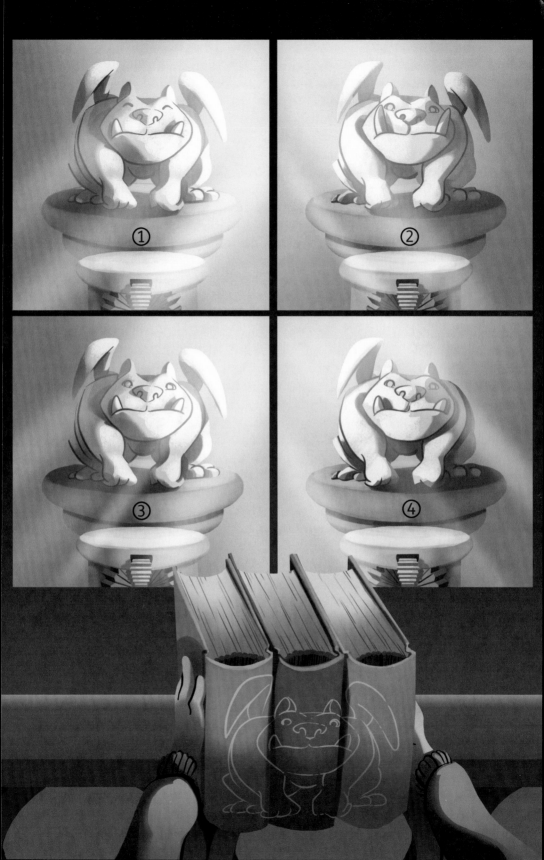

THE MYSTERIOUS STAIRCASE

Marvin pointed at statue number three.

"That's the one."

Sneaking back downstairs, we made our way to the statue. I held the books over its tray and took a deep breath.

"This is it," I said. "Ready for adventure?"

Lilli and Marvin nodded. I let go of the

books. *Click.* A deep rumbling arose.

Everything started to shake.

"Uh-oh," Lilli said, panic in her eyes.

Suddenly, a part of the library floor sank

into the ground, revealing a staircase.

Dust filled the room. People coughed
and covered their eyes.

"Everyone stand back," Mrs. Wiseone
shouted.

In the chaos, someone bumped into
Marvin's chair. It tipped over, and his
backpack fell off. The ground kept
shaking. Marvin's bag shook with it.

Then it fell right into the hole.

"Froggy!" Marvin shouted and dashed

down the stairs.

"Marvin, wait!" I yelled.

I looked around. Mrs. Wiseone was busy

helping the other kids.

"We have to go help him," Lilli said.

She took my hand and we ran down.

"Marvin!" I shouted.

"Here," Marvin called. "Froggy is okay."

The frog was, but what about *us*? Where

were we? My heart was pounding. Then

it got even worse.

From behind us, we heard a familiar rumbling. I turned and saw the staircase rising upward again! Seconds later, our way back was cut off.

"Uh-oh," Lilli said.

"The hole has closed. The library floor has settled back into place," I said.

"There's light over there," Lilli whispered.

"Please let this be a way out," I said, running toward it.

The light shone through little holes in a wall. I could smell fresh air. We pushed against the stones. They wouldn't budge.

"I think we are in trouble," I said.

"Look," Marvin said. He pointed at a wall with an inscription and images.

"I carry thoughts but have no mind," I read. "Those who care about me give me away to those who rip me apart."

"A riddle. One of the images must show the solution," Lilli said.

Marvin nodded. "Yup. That one."

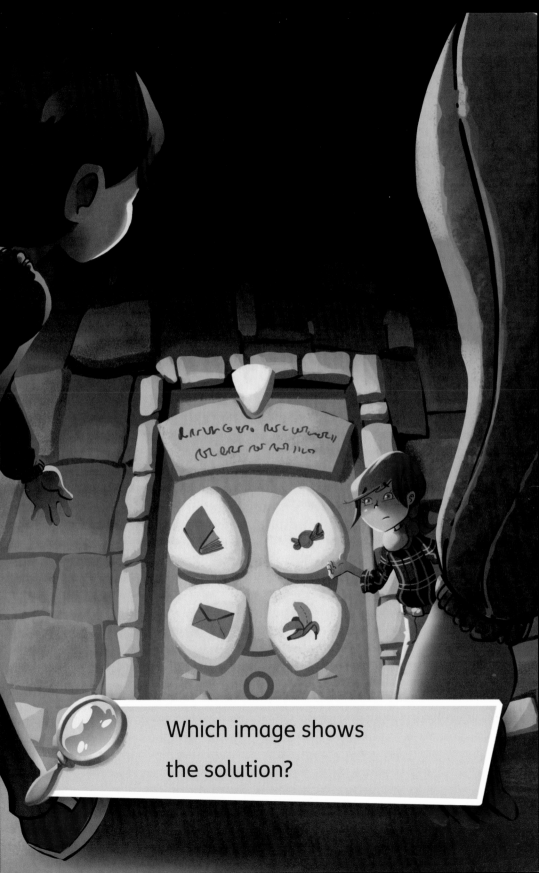

Which image shows
the solution?

BACKALLEY ONE

"You give away an envelope so someone can read what's inside. And you tear it apart to open it," Marvin said. He pushed the button. We heard a *click* and a note fell out of a small slot above us.

"Deliver to Backalley One," I read it.

"What is Backalley One?"

40

Suddenly, the wall that wouldn't budge slid away all by itself. Blinding sunlight hit our faces. Before us lay a muddy alley lined with tall buildings.

"We made it," Marvin shouted, jumping up and down. "We're out!"

"Look at that. This is so unreal," I said.

"A secret passageway!" Marvin said.

"Wow," Lilli said. "Look how far it runs."

Marvin picked up his backpack, and we set off down the alley.

Behind us, the stone wall slid shut again.

"None of the houses have windows or doors," Lilli said. "We must be looking at the back side of buildings."

"Incredible," I said nervously. "There must be a way out, right?"

Several buildings down, we came to a crossroads. Small golden arrows engraved with letters hung on the brick walls at the corner.

"BONE," Lilli read. "That could stand for Backalley One. We should follow it."

Lilli was right. Several crossroads later, we came to a door—the first we'd seen. The sign near it read: BACKALLEY ONE—CLUB FOR ADVENTURERS AND DETECTIVES.

"A secret club," I said. "Maybe that's what my brother wanted me to find."

"This all seems strange," Lilli said.

"What kind of person joins a club like this?"

A hanging cord led up to a golden bell. Nervously, I grabbed it.

"I guess we're about to find out," I said.

Lilli and Marvin hesitated at first. Then they nodded. I pulled the cord and the bell rang out.

A friendly-looking man opened the door.

"And who might you be?" he asked.

I handed him the note.

"Solved the riddle, did ya? Let me see you.

Huh. Three kids and . . . a frog?"

"Yes, sir," Marvin said. "I helped him get

well after he lost a leg."

"You've got a kind heart, young man. Well

I'm glad it's you kids and not another

runner. Our runners deliver messages.

They rang the bell shortly before you did!"

He paused and looked at us expectantly.

I hesitated. Then I said, "I'm sorry, sir.

But I don't think anyone else rang the bell

recently."

What made Timmi sure no one else had recently rung the bell?

A TEST OF WITS

"Look at that mud puddle. Anyone who came through would have left footprints. But there are only three sets—from us," I said.

"A keen observer," the man said. "I'm Boris. Come in. I'll show you around."

We cautiously followed Boris inside.

"Our club was founded over a hundred

years ago," he said. "We solve the mysteries no one else can."

Boris led us to a room. "These are our researchers. They help us solve our most difficult cases. Not that it's all paperwork. Our missions take us all over the world. To do our work, one must understand history, archaeology . . . underwater exploration."

"Underwater exploration?" I asked.

Boris nodded. "Are you by any chance a
scuba diver?"

I shook my head.

"Pity," Boris said, moving on. He opened
another door. "Ah, yes. Our Common Hall."

As we entered, a girl ran past us,
shouting, "I've been robbed!"

To my surprise, everyone stayed calm.

50

"It's their daily exercise," Boris explained. "Every day one student presents a made-up case to the class. A chance to sharpen their wits and hone their skills."

"So no one was robbed for real?" Lilli asked.

Boris smiled. "No. It's just a test. But today, it is *your* test."

"Our test?" I asked. "Why would you want to test us?"

"The truth is, we have been testing you all day. Just getting here was a test. But now we must find out if you have what it takes to join us. Pass the last test and we will offer you a future of education, training, and companionship. Full of mysteries to solve. Full of adventure."

"Why us?" Lilli asked.

"One of our members recommended you," Boris said. "He believes in who you are. Clever, talented, and kind."

"Who recommended us?" I asked.

"I expect you know who it is," Boris answered. "He would be very proud if you were to join Backalley One."

"Tom!" I said. "My brother is a member of Backalley One?"

Boris smiled. "Now then, time to decide. Shall we go on or will you go home?"

"We'll take the test," Lilli said.

"So you are the determined one," Boris noted. "Well then, let's begin."

We all followed the girl who claimed to have been robbed to her bedroom.

"I had just left this room when I heard glass break," she said. "I raced back in, but it was too late. Someone had broken the window from outside to open the door, stolen my notes, and run back out."

"Not true," Lilli said. "Her story is a lie."

What made Lilli sure the girl was lying?

THE CHASE IS ON

"The pieces of broken glass are outside," Lilli said. "If the window had been smashed from outside, they would be inside."

The girl smirked. "You caught me lying. But can you catch me running?"

Just like that, the girl took off.

Marvin handed his frog to Boris. "Can you hold Froggy, please, sir?" he said.

Then we ran after her.

We found ourselves in a courtyard.

Ahead of us, the girl ducked down an

alley. We reached it just in time to see

a door close. Marvin hauled open the

door and we ran through. Before us

was a room with high walls and people

practicing free climbing.

The girl slipped through another door.

We followed her into a gigantic gym.

In the corner, a door slammed shut.

I ran through, then skidded

to a stop.

In front of us was a pool with divers practicing underwater exploration. Two more steps and I would have fallen in. We edged around the water and through the only other door.

We were back in the courtyard, but the girl was nowhere to be seen.

"She went that way," Boris said. He pointed to three doors. "The question is, were you paying attention when you ran across the courtyard earlier? You did get a glimpse of these doors then. Which one did she use?"

We looked at them. At first I had no idea. But then I remembered and saw it. "That one," I said, pointing.

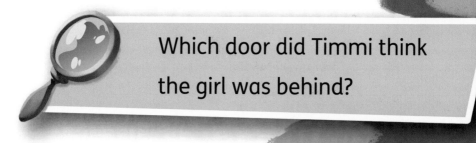

Which door did Timmi think the girl was behind?

"The ivy is stuck in the top of the left door," I said. "It didn't look like that before."

I pulled it open. The girl behind it clapped her hands and smiled.

Boris nodded. "You solved the case."

"And made me proud," a familiar voice said behind me.

I turned and saw my brother Tom smiling at me. "Tom!" I yelled and jumped into his arms.

Tom knelt down to me. "I knew you'd make it," he whispered.

"It wasn't just me," I said.

"I know," he said. "It never is. None of us can get far without good friends by our sides."

"Tom, these kids formed a great team," Boris said. "They are kind, determined and smart."

"So admit all of them," Tom said.

"Indeed," Boris said. "Indeed. Lilli, Marvin, Timmi. I hereby declare you early apprentices of Backalley One."

"Sounds awesome!" I said, smiling from ear to ear.

Marvin bobbed up and down, clapping his hands.

"That's how I started out, too," Tom said. "I solved a different riddle when I was your age."

"Apprentices? What do apprentices do?"
Lilli asked.

"You will continue your normal everyday
life," Boris said. "But from time to time,
you will be given small tasks to help
Backalley One."

"Small but important," Tom added.

"Your first task is to form your own club
for adventurers and detectives," Boris
continued.

"Helping others is the best way to prepare yourselves for what lies ahead," Tom said and handed me a book. "The Backalley One Handbook. It's full of useful tips!"

"But now we need to reunite you with your class," Boris said. "Marvin, here is your frog back."

Tom guided us out to the exit.

"The library is that way," he said, pointing.

"Wait," Lilli said. "People saw the hidden staircase in the library. They will find the room below. And the secret alleyways behind the buildings. They will find Backalley One."

Tom shook his head. "They will only find what we want them to."

"But what are we supposed to tell everyone?" Lilli asked.

"Tell everyone the truth," Tom said. "If someone comes knocking, we will handle it. Don't worry."

"That was so cool!" Marvin said. "Did you see all those training rooms?"

I nodded. "I wonder what mysteries they solve."

"Whatever they are, it looks like we've got a whole lot of adventures coming our way," Lilli said.

Marvin clapped his hands. "What should we call our club? Shadows of the Fox? No. The Stealthy Foxes!"

Beside me, Lilli snickered.

"Oh, I bet you'd like something boring," Marvin said.

"Actually," Lilli said, "how about **The Young Explorers?**"

"Um, okay," Marvin said. "Not bad."

"I like it," I said.

I grinned as we set off. Each step took us closer to our next adventure, and I couldn't wait!

THE
END
(FOR NOW)

The students at Backalley One strive to solve mysteries, ancient and modern. To be successful, they need to know a lot. Here is a collection of fascinating facts taught at Backalley One that relate to this book's adventure.

Pssst. Get this book's Success Badge!

Collect all the letters displayed in the emblems on the following pages. Rearrange the letters to form two words. Then enter the words in the "Badges" section on timmitobbson.com to download your Success Badge. Print it out and paste it in its place on the first page to show you solved every mystery and read all the facts and tips for young explorers!

Backalley One uses a secret network of alleyways. In "ancient" times, alleyways provided shortcuts, many of which were secret, too.

One interesting example of this is a city in France. The city is called Lyon. Here, over 400 hidden alleyways are said to exist. They wind their way through the city, running behind, below, and even above its buildings.

Among other purposes, they helped the people of Lyon hide from invaders.

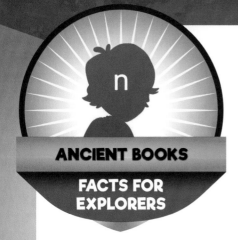

Old books can be fascinating. You never know what you will find inside. But the older a book, the more fragile it is. Oils from your fingers can damage them, so it is important to wash your hands. Bindings can crack, so books should be looked at on a book cradle. And pages must be turned very carefully, with special tools. Some rare books are worth millions of dollars.

Throughout history, riddles have played a big part in stories and legends. One famous story is that of the Sphinx—a mythical creature said to guard the entrance to the city of Thebes.

In order for travelers to enter, they had to solve this difficult riddle: "Which creature first walks on four legs, then on two, and finally on three?" Use a mirror to read the solution:

The answer is „human.“ We crawl on all fours as babies, walk on two legs as adults, and use a walking stick as a „third leg," in old age.

Scuba diving is a hard skill to learn, but valuable to any adventurer. This is why it is taught at Backalley One. Many sunken ships have been explored for treasure. One famous case is the ship of Blackbeard the pirate.

Blackbeard roamed the sea in the early 18th century. In 1996, divers exploring off the coast of North Carolina, USA, found his sunken ship and many artifacts. Experts think 3 million shipwrecks may be lost at sea. There is plenty of work to do for explorers.

History is full of famous explorers. Have you heard about Ferdinand Magellan? He became the first person to sail all the way around the world.

Today, there are still many caves and underwater areas that have not yet been fully explored—or even found. In 2018, an enormous cave was discovered in Canada that, until recently, had been covered in ice and snow!

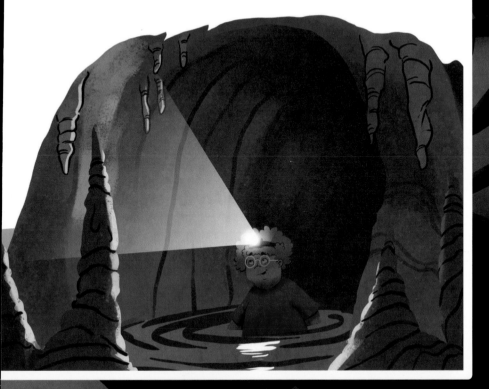

Young apprentices get the classified

Backalley One Handbook. Now *you* can apply

its secrets and become a Young Explorer!

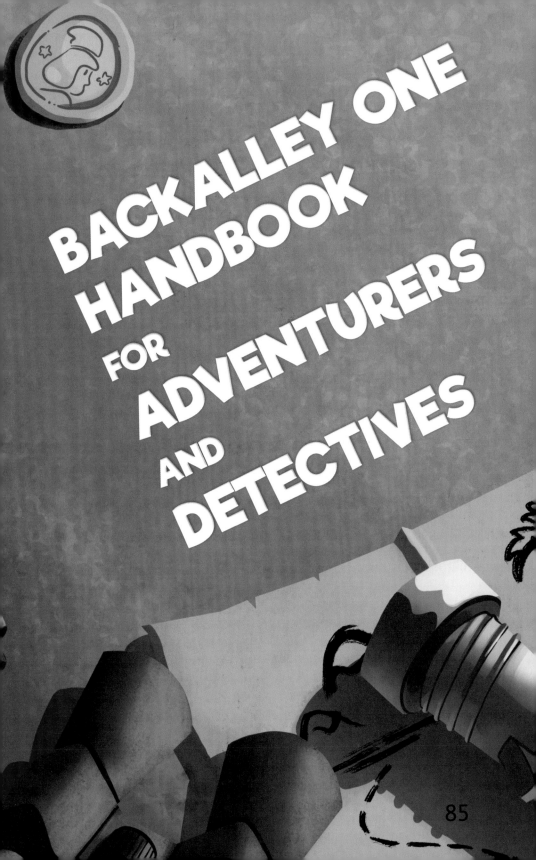

BACKALLEY ONE HANDBOOK FOR ADVENTURERS AND DETECTIVES

FINGERPRINTS

Police use a special powder to help them collect fingerprints. It is harder to do it on your own, but you can try! You need transparent tape, a fine powder like baking soda, a brush, some butter or oil, and colored paper.

1. Use butter to grease a finger and press it

against a glass. You should see the fingerprint on the glass.

2. Use the brush to spread some baking soda over the fingerprint.

3. Now, carefully brush away any excess baking soda.

4. Put a strip of your tape over the print. Don't let it slip.

5. Remove the tape and gently stick it onto the colored paper. Now you should see the print. Try again if it does not work the first time around.

To find Backalley One, Timmi and his friends followed an arrow. Of course, everybody knows what an arrow means. But you can leave signs for your friends that aren't well known. You can use twigs, crayons, or little stones.

You can either develop your own set of signs or use these scout trail markers:

 "Go this way"

 "We split up"

 "Follow opposite direction"

 "Wrong way"

 "Danger"

Would you like to write secret messages? Here is one way to do it. Write some random phrases. Next, within the phrases mark the letters that spell out your secret message. Finally, mark one random letter between each of the letters you already marked. These other letters are there only as a decoy.

Following this code, can you read this secret message?

What <u>a</u> nice li<u>tt</u>le p<u>u</u>p<u>py</u>.

I li<u>k</u>e to play with <u>my</u> dog.

<u>A</u>ll th<u>e</u> <u>t</u>ime<u>!</u>

Use a mirror to read the solution:
Help me!

Imagine you get stranded on a desert island. You need to drink, but the water from the ocean is too salty. How can you make drinking water?

You need a cup (A), bucket or bowl (B), a stone (C), tin or plastic foil (D), tape or a thread.

C

B

A

D

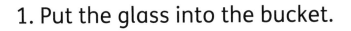

1. Put the glass into the bucket.

2. Pour saltwater into the bucket, but not too much—you don't want the glass to float.

3. Stretch the tin foil over the bucket and hold it in place using tape or by wrapping a thread around the bucket.

4. Put the stone in the center of the foil.

5. Now put the bucket in a warm, sunny place and wait. As the water evaporates, the vapor will reach the tin foil and stream to its lowest point (the middle), then drop into the glass.

6. After a few hours you will find drinkable water in the cup.

How do you know if your room has been searched while you were gone?

One way to find out is to set little traps. Take a long hair (or a very thin thread) and attach some tape on each end. Make sure you use plenty of tape, so the hair cannot come loose by itself. Stick it inside a drawer that an intruder may search (see illustration). If someone opens the drawer, it will tear or come loose.

95

Pssst. Here are some hints!

Page 17

Look at the lines under the three words. One of the lines is interrupted because the page is torn. What do you see on the page beneath? What does that tell you?

Page 25

Lilli is looking at the spines of the books. She sees a set of lines that don't make sense on their own. But imagine the spines next to each other. What do you see?

Page 30

Marvin is comparing the spines of the books to the statues. What is different about each statue? Which one is an exact match?

Page 39

Which of the pictures shows something that you rip open? Which contains thoughts? Marvin solves the puzzle by ruling out one button at a time, until only one is left.

Page 47

Timmi is looking at the footprints on the ground. What do they tell you about what did or did not happen lately?

Page 55

Lilli is looking at the glass on the ground outside. What do the fallen shards tell you about how the glass pane in the door was broken?

Page 60

Timmi is looking at the ivy above the doors. Something has changed since the first time he saw those doors. Can you find what it is?